THE HE

27-12-11

Blizzard

SADDLEBACK
EDUCATIONAL PUBLISHING

X

T H E H E I G H T S

Blizzard   River

Camp   Sail

Crash   Score

Dive   Swamp

Neptune   Twister

Original text by Ed Hansen
Adapted by Mary Kate Doman

SADDLEBACK
EDUCATIONAL PUBLISHING
www.sdlback.com

Copyright © 2012 by Saddleback Educational Publishing
All rights reserved. No part of this book may be reproduced in any form or
by any means, electronic or mechanical, including photocopying, recording,
scanning, or by any information storage and retrieval system without the
written permission of the publisher.

ISBN-13: 978-1-61651-623-9
ISBN-10: 1-61651-623-2
eBook: 978-1-61247-308-6

Printed in Guangzhou, China
0611/CA21100644

16 15 14 13 12   1 2 3 4 5 6

Chapter 1

Rafael got the call an hour ago. It was his office. They needed his help on a job. He had to get there right away. It was a last-minute trip. And the kids were going too. It was a school holiday. And a great time for some family fun. After Rafael's quick meeting, they were going skiing.

The family got lucky. There were four seats on the next plane. They had 15 minutes before they had to leave the Heights for the airport. Everyone packed fast. Ana Silva stuffed warm clothes into everyone's bag. She didn't want anyone to freeze!

"Come on, Mom! We aren't going to the North Pole," Antonio said.

"I know. I want to make sure you're warm. It's cold in the mountains," said Ana. "And Antonio, here are some snacks for the plane. It's a long flight."

"Thanks, Mom!" Antonio said.

Ana gave Antonio a bag filled with food. Then she gave him a hug.

Rafael looked at Ana.

"I wish you'd come too," Rafael said.

"Just be safe this time," said Ana. "Don't ski in a blizzard." She winked.

Then he and the kids left. Ana looked out the window. She watched the car drive away. She looked like she might change her mind. Maybe it was time for a little adventure…

Chapter 2

The Silvas ate burgers and fries in the airport. But they had to eat fast. Their flight was going to board.

"Good thing Mom isn't here," Franco said. "She'd make us eat vegetables."

Rafael smiled. "The only vegetable here is your pickle. And I wish your mom was here," said Rafael.

Antonio ordered too much food.

He stuffed fries and a burger in his bag for later.

"*Gross*!" Lilia said.

"What? They taste good cold," said Antonio. He rubbed his stomach.

On the plane, the kids ate snacks. But Rafael wasn't hungry. He gave his pretzels and peanuts to Lilia. She didn't want them. But she saved them for later.

"We fly into Salt Lake City, Utah. Then we'll go to the Grand Teton Mountains in Wyoming. We're skiing in Jackson Hole," Rafael said.

"Hey, Dad, are there any animals in the Grand Tetons?" Antonio asked.

"Yes," said Rafael. "Mountain lions are very dangerous. If a mountain lion attacks... Forget it!

They have huge claws and teeth. And they're very strong. But they don't often attack people."

Antonio looked a little upset. He didn't like scary animals. But he knew that mountain lions didn't usually attack people. It made him feel a little better.

Soon the plane landed. The Silvas were tired after the long flight. Rafael got the rental car. It was dark. They didn't see much of Salt Lake City. Everyone fell asleep when they got to the hotel.

Rafael got up early the next morning. He called Ana. They talked quietly. The kids didn't wake up. He promised to call Ana from Jackson Hole.

The meeting was only two hours. Everyone was ready when it was over. They wanted to get to Jackson Hole.

Rafael pulled out a map. "Look," he said. "We'll go north. Then we'll head into Wyoming. We'll be skiing this afternoon."

Chapter 3

It was a beautiful day. A few clouds were in the sky. And the sun was shining. The Silvas drove through the valley. They were excited to see the Grand Tetons.

Lilia saw sharp points of rock. She looked worried.

"Is *that* were we're going to ski?" Lilia asked.

"Don't worry," said Rafael. "That's

much higher than where we're going. The ski slopes aren't near the top."

"There are coyote, moose, black bears, and deer up there. We may see some of them. Not any bears though. They sleep all winter," Rafael said. "We'll see some elk. They look like big deer. Every winter they come here. They are snacks for the mountain lions!"

He stopped the car.

Rafael pointed. "Look over there! Moose!" he shouted.

They saw three tall animals. Their heads looked too big for their bodies. Lilia laughed. She thought their horns looked like trees on their heads.

"Weird," Antonio said.

Then a herd of elk came out of

the woods. There were 15 elk in the herd. Elk were much prettier than moose. Each one was looking for food. Before he scared them, Rafael drove away.

The land began to rise. They drove higher and higher. The sky looked cloudy. Soon they saw snowflakes.

"I hope it doesn't snow too much to ski," Franco said.

"Don't worry," Rafael said. "I looked at the weather report. It's going to be sunny."

A beautiful lake was below. It was a greenish blue. And the water was very clear. Antonio looked at the lake. He loved science. He just learned about the Ice Age in school.

He knew it was a glacier lake.

"That lake was made by a glacier," said Antonio.

"What's a glacier?" Lilia asked.

"The world got very cold thousands of years ago. Ice covered the Earth. It was called the Ice Age. Most of the ice is melted now. But it left some lakes. This is one of them," Antonio said.

"Cool. Can the Ice Age happen again?" Lilia asked.

"Maybe. But not for thousands of years," said Antonio.

It snowed harder. Rafael drove on.

"Are you sure it's sunny in Jackson Hole?" Franco asked.

"That was the report," Rafael said. "Franco, find a weather channel."

Chapter 4

Franco looked for the weather report. But his cell phone didn't have a signal.

Lilia looked out the window.

"Look! The sun is gone," she said. "The sky is cloudy and gray."

"Yeah, it's getting dark," Antonio said.

The light snow got heavier. The road was slippery. Soon snow covered the ground. The car struggled to get up the hill. It got hard to see. Everything was white.

Franco tuned the radio. He found a station.

"A sudden snowstorm is coming in fast. Police want everyone off the roads. Repeat: This is a very bad storm," the announcer warned.

"I'm turning around," said Rafael. "Let's go back. We can ski tomorrow."

The kids were upset. But they knew their father was right.

Rafael couldn't find a place to turn around. He hadn't noticed that the road had become narrow.

"That's weird," Rafael said. "We were on a main road. Did I turn off by mistake? I think we're on a side road."

Finally, Rafael found a place to turn. Now he was driving downhill. He drove very slowly. The car slid from side to side. They came to a very steep hill.

"I remember this place," Franco said. "We're on the top of a cliff. It's where we saw the glacier lake below."

The snow fell even faster. No one could see at all. They couldn't see where the road was. Everyone was scared.

"I have to stop the car," said Rafael. "There's no choice!"

Rafael put on the brakes. But nothing happened. The car couldn't stop on the slippery snow.

The car picked up speed. It went faster and faster. It was out of control! Rafael struggled with the steering wheel. But it didn't work. It was hopeless!

They couldn't see anything but white. Now they had no idea where the cliff was. The car hit something and stopped. Lilia and Antonio screamed.

Everyone was quiet for a minute. No one knew what had happened. But they were all happy that they didn't fall off the cliff!

"Are you all okay?" Rafael asked. His voice sounded weak.

The kids were scared. But they weren't hurt.

Lilia began to cry. She couldn't stop. Her body was shaking hard. Antonio put his arms around her.

Franco patted her head.

"It's okay. We're not really hurt, Lilia," Antonio said.

"I want Mom," Lilia cried.

"We'll be fine," Franco said. "Don't worry."

The boys kept on talking to Lilia. Then Franco realized his dad hadn't said much.

Chapter 5

"Dad, are you okay?" Franco asked.

"Not really. My leg is stuck under the wheel," said Rafael.

His voice sounded weak. It sounded like he was in pain. Then Rafael let out a groan.

"My ankle is broken. I'm sure. It hurts a lot. But I'll be okay when we get help," Rafael said. "I'm not going to be of much use. You guys are going to have to get us out of here."

All three Silva kids worried about their dad. Lilia stopped crying. Antonio and Franco closely looked at Rafael. He was pale and sweating. His body was bent over the steering wheel. They had to move him.

They still couldn't see out of the windows. Wind shook the car from side to side.

"What should we do?" Lilia asked. She had never been so scared. Her dad was always the one helping her.

"First we need to move you to the back. Then you can lie down," Franco said.

"Great," said Rafael. "I'll pass out if I don't lie down. But you'll have to move me without opening the doors. The wind is too strong. We won't have shelter if the door blows off.

The kids lowered the seats. Lilia held Rafael's leg. The two boys rolled him onto the back seat.

"I feel much better already," Rafael sighed. "Thank you."

He looked much better too. The car rocked in the wind. The kids talked about what to do. Franco and Antonio stayed in the front. Lilia sat in the back with Rafael. This gave them more room. But the car was still tight. And now they were very cold.

"Let's turn on the engine. We could put on the heat," Antonio said.

"I wish we could," said Rafael.

"But there could be snow in the tailpipe. It would push poisonous fumes into the car. We can't take that chance."

"But I'm r-r-really c-c-cold," Lilia said.

"Look through the bags," said Franco. "Mom packed all those warm clothes."

Lilia opened the bags. She grabbed scarves, hats, gloves, and sweaters. They put on everything. No one cared if they looked silly.

"Do you think Mom knew this would happen?" Lilia asked.

"No way!" said Antonio. "She wouldn't have let us come. She just likes us to be ready for emergencies."

Then Franco said, "I'm getting

hungry."

All of them were hungry! Antonio pulled out his cold fries and burger. Lilia didn't think they were gross anymore. Lilia had the pretzels and peanuts from the plane. She shared them with everyone too. It wasn't much. But at least it was something!

There was nothing to do but sleep. They weren't going to freeze. But they were very cold! It was going to be a long night.

No one had much room. Lilia slept on the bump on the back floor. Franco and Antonio slept sitting up. Everyone was thirsty.

Lilia was scared. "I wish Mom was here," she said again.

"I don't," Antonio said. "Then

she'd be stuck here too!"

"We all feel the same," said Rafael. "In our hearts we want Mom to be here. But in our heads we're glad she's not."

Soon the Silvas fell asleep. Everyone wondered the same thing. How close was their car to the cliff?

Chapter 6

Everyone woke early. Lilia looked out the window. She was afraid the car would be buried in snow. But it wasn't. It had stopped snowing. The sun was shining.

Now they could see. The car was at the bottom of a hill. A high peak was above them. Rafael could see it from the back seat. He stared up at it.

They couldn't see the cliff

anywhere. But they knew it was close. Everything was so white. It was hard to tell where things were.

They knew how dangerous their situation was. Being stranded was bad enough. But in the snowy mountains, it was *very* bad. Especially when no one knew they were missing.

Franco and Antonio dug out one side of the car. They used Franco's ski helmet for a shovel. Snow went up to the windows. It took a lot of work. But they finally cleared the tailpipe.

Franco climbed back into the car. He tried to start it.

"Please start," Lilia cried. "I'm so cold!"

Nothing happened. So Franco

tried again. The engine didn't make a sound.

"It's not working," said Franco.

"Don't worry. We're not going to freeze," said Rafael. "We'll be cold though."

"Well, so much for that," Franco said. "On to our next problem. Where can we get food?"

"I don't think we're going to find any," said Rafael. "But it's okay. We can live for days without food. It won't be fun. But we can do it."

"It won't be fun at all," said Antonio.

Then he remembered something.

"Wait a minute!" shouted Antonio. "We do have food. Mom gave me a bag of snacks for the plane."

Antonio pulled everything out of his bag. At the bottom was a paper bag. Antonio tore it open. He couldn't wait to look inside. The bag was filled. It had peanut butter sandwiches, apples, and cookies!

"Mom's sure doing a lot to help us. And she's not even here!" Lilia said.

They'd all been thirsty. But it was worse after eating peanut butter. Lack of water was their biggest problem.

"We could eat snow," said Lilia. "It will melt in our mouths and turn to water."

"It doesn't work that way," said Rafael. "Eating snow makes you thirstier."

"Can we melt it and then drink

it?" asked Lilia.

"Yes!" Franco said. "We can use small branches. We can light them with the car's lighter."

Rafael frowned. "We don't have anything to melt the snow in," he said.

Everyone looked around.

"I know!" Antonio yelled. "Why don't we use a hubcap?"

Their plan worked. Antonio cut some branches. He put them next to the car. Then Franco lit them with the lighter.

Lilia filled a hubcap with snow. When the snow melted, it turned to water. They passed the hubcap around. Everybody took a sip.

"Not bad," Rafael said.

The small fire even kept them warm. So far they were surviving.

Chapter 7

Even though they were warm now,
Rafael was worried. No one knew
where they were. How could they be
rescued?

"You know, Dad, there's only one
thing to do," Franco said.

"I know," Rafael replied. "I keep
thinking about it. I can't think of
another way. You have to get help.
You have to ski down to town. It's

31

about 20 miles. I hate to make you
do it."

"I can do it, Dad. Don't worry,"
said Franco.

He lifted weights. He ran every
day. Franco was in great shape. And
he was a good skier. Franco was sure
he could ski 20 miles.

Franco had to leave right away.
It got dark early. He put on his
warm clothes, hat, and gloves. Lilia
wrapped her scarf around him.
Antonio gave him extra gloves.

"Come on," Franco said. "You're
worse than Mom!"

Antonio gave Franco the last two
peanut butter sandwiches and an
apple.

Franco was finally ready. It was

time for him to take off. Rafael gave Franco a hug. Franco could tell that he was worried.

He said good-bye to Antonio and Lilia. Then he turned toward the road. At least he hoped it was the road. It was hard to tell with all the white.

Antonio and Lilia watched him go. They were proud of their brother. Franco turned around. He gave them a thumbs-up.

"That must mean he found the road," Lilia said.

They watched him ski away. He looked smaller as he skied off. Finally, he disappeared.

The wind blew in Franco's face. Everything was white. It was hard to see the road. Franco made a lot of wrong turns. It was very tiring.

Franco saw a lot of animals. He saw eagles soaring in the sky. Then he saw a herd of elk. He also saw tracks in the snow. They were big. Franco guessed they were mountain lion tracks.

Franco remembered what his dad said about them. Mountain lions didn't often attack people. But Franco was a little worried. Rafael didn't say mountain lions *never* attacked people. He still didn't want to see one.

Franco stopped for a sandwich. He was very tired. He'd been skiing for hours. The blowing snow hurt his face.

The mountain peaks rose high in the west. Franco knew what that meant. Soon they would block out the sun. It would quickly get dark. He knew he'd be in the mountains overnight.

It was around 20 degrees. It would be a lot colder at night. But he knew what he had to do.

First he needed to find a tree. There had to be a mound of snow piled next to the tree. Then he had to dig a tunnel in the snow. He would make an igloo. It was his only chance to live through the night. Or he would freeze to death.

Franco used his skis as shovels. He dug until he was very tired. He could hardly stand. At last he finished. The igloo was ready. He wiggled in. Then he filled in the opening with snow. He left a small hole for air. He knew he would be cold.

Franco was so tired. He quickly fell asleep.

Chapter 8

"I'm going out in the snow," Antonio said. "Maybe I can find out where we are."

"Don't go too far. And be careful," said Lilia. "You still don't know where that cliff is."

Lilia watched Antonio walk away. He walked slowly. It was hard for him to walk. The snow was very deep. Then Antonio disappeared. It happened fast.

Lilia jumped out of the car. She went over to where she last saw him. She looked down. It was the cliff! The valley was far below.

Antonio was a few feet from the top. He clung to a small tree. It wouldn't hold his weight long. Antonio's feet dangled in the air! Lilia didn't know what to do.

"Lilia, help me!" Antonio yelled. "I can't hold on much longer."

Antonio's arms shook. The little tree was breaking. Antonio wasn't far down. Lilia could touch him. But she was too small to pull Antonio up. If she tried, he would drag her over the edge.

"Hold on, Antonio," Lilia yelled.

"Don't give up! I'll be right back."

Lilia ran back to the car. She told her dad what happened.

Rafael quickly got out of the car. He dragged himself to the cliff. Soon Rafael got to the edge. He looked down at Antonio.

Lilia held her breath. Rafael leaned over and reached down. He grabbed Antonio's arm.

"Antonio, keep looking up," said Rafael. "Don't look down! Grab my arm!"

Antonio reached up.

"Now let go of the tree," said Rafael. "Grab my arm with your other hand."

But Antonio looked down. He froze in terror.

"I can't let go!" Antonio cried.

"Antonio!" Rafael yelled. "You have to let go! The tree is breaking!"

Antonio was frozen with fear. He couldn't let go.

"Close your eyes," Rafael said.

Antonio closed his eyes. Then he let go. And he grabbed his dad's arm.

Rafael pulled Antonio up very slowly.

Lilia cheered. Her brother was safe.

Antonio's life-or-death fall had worn them out. No one felt like talking. They just sat in the car. The day seemed very long. But they needed the rest. The cold and hunger took a lot out of them.

Chapter 9

The next morning Franco shoveled away the snow. Then he crawled out of his igloo.

He put on his skis. Then he headed back down the hill.

Franco knew he had to get help fast. He was his family's only chance. He skied down the hill at full speed.

Five minutes later, he saw something strange. A dark patch was moving toward him. Now he could see that it was a herd of elk. They were in a panic. He had to get out of the way. If not, they would crush him.

Franco could feel the ground shake. He hit the ground. And he rolled down the mountain. He saw hundreds of legs coming toward him. He covered his head with his arms. The elk missed him by a few feet. Then they were gone.

Franco wondered what happened to scare the elk.

Back at the car, Rafael, Antonio, and Lilia heard a rumbling. It got louder. The ground shook.

"Avalanche!" Rafael yelled.

The avalanche only lasted a few minutes. But it seemed like hours.

When it was over everything was quiet. Too quiet.

Antonio looked out the window. He couldn't see anything.

"Do you think we're buried?" Antonio asked.

"No!" Lilia said. "I see sky. The avalanche missed us."

But behind the car was a wall of snow. It was 10 times higher than the car! They would have been buried alive if the avalanche was any closer! They were lucky. And everyone knew it.

Rafael hoped Franco was okay. He was their only chance. They wouldn't make it much longer.

Chapter 10

Franco rested in the snow. He was
tired and scared. He got away from
the elk. But he still had a long way
to go.

Franco got up. Before long, Franco
heard a noise. It was running water.
It was coming from under the snow.
He made it to the lake! Now he
needed to find the road.

Franco looked closer. He found

the bridge! The road had to be close.

The bridge was long. But he had to make it over. He was tired. He couldn't move without pain. Franco didn't think he could go on.

Lilia, Antonio, and Rafael were still in the car. They were trying to play a word game. But no one was into it.

Then Lilia heard something. At first, she thought it was another avalanche. But it sounded different. It was a humming sound. It had to be a plane!

Everyone looked out the windows. But there was no plane in sight. But something moved toward them on the ground.

"Franco got through!" Rafael yelled.

Antonio and Lilia cheered when three snowmobiles finally got to the car. Franco jumped off the first snowmobile.

"You're safe! The avalanche didn't get you!" he cried.

Another driver was using a radio.

The last snowmobile driver ran over to the car. It was Ana! She grabbed Lilia and Antonio. She gave them a big hug.

"Mom!" Lilia yelled.

"What?" Antonio asked. "Where did you come from?"

"Your dad didn't call from Jackson Hole. It made me worry," Ana said. "I called and found out you never got there. Then I heard about the storm. I just had to make sure you were all okay!"

Then Ana held out a paper bag. Antonio saw the fast-food logo on it.

"Food, sweet!" yelled Antonio. "Mom, you rock."

He ripped the bag open. It was filled with hot burgers and fries.

Then Ana walked over to the car. She opened the door. Rafael was still on the back seat.

"Rough couple of nights, huh?" she asked.

"Ana," Rafael sighed. "I can't believe you're here. You helped us more than you know. Without being here, you fed us and kept us warm!"

"You have the worst luck on these trips, Rafael," she said. "How's that ankle?"

"It's been better," said Rafael. "Hey, kids, start digging out the car. We have a big day of skiing tomorrow!"

Ana and the kids looked at Rafael. He started to laugh. He knew he wasn't going to be skiing for a long time. Everyone else joined him.

The next day the Silvas stayed *inside* the ski lodge. They'd had enough excitement for one trip!